Dream Catcher

Story Keeper Series
Book 5

For the Children of Perryville, AR

Dave and Pat Sargent (*left*) are longtime residents of Prairie Grove, Arkansas. Dave, a fourth-generation dairy farmer, began writing in early December 1990. Pat, a former teacher, began writing in the fourth grade. They enjoy the outdoors and have a real love for animals.

Sue Rogers (*right*) returned to her beloved Mississippi after retirement. She shared books with children for more than thirty years. These stories fulfill a dream of writing books—to continue the sharing.

Dream Catcher

Story Keeper Series
Book 5

By Dave and Pat Sargent
and Sue Rogers

Beyond "The End"
By Sue Rogers

Illustrated by Jane Lenoir

Ozark Publishing, Inc.
P.O. Box 228
Prairie Grove, AR 72753

Cataloging-in-Publication Data

Sargent, Dave, 1941–
    Dream catcher / by Dave and
Pat Sargent and Sue Rogers ; illustrated by
Jane Lenoir.—Prairie Grove, AR : Ozark
Publishing, c2004.
        p. cm. (Story keeper series ; 5)

        "Be strong"—Cover.
        SUMMARY: Kohana was preparing for
his first buffalo hunt. He needed help dealing
with evil dreams before it was too late.
        ISBN 1-56763-911-9 (hc)
                1-56763-912-7 (pbk)

        1. Indians of North America—Juvenile
fiction. 2. Lakota Indians—Juvenile fiction.
3. Dreams—Juvenile fiction. [1. Native
Americans—United States—Fiction.
2. Lakota Indians—Fiction. 3. Dreams—
Fiction.] I. Sargent, Pat, 1936– II. Rogers,
Sue, 1933– III. Lenoir, Jane, 1950– ill.
IV. Title. V. Series
        PZ7.S243Dr 2004
        [Fic]—dc21   2003090089

iv

Inspired by

all who have a dream catcher
above their bed to sift their dreams.

Dedicated to

Leonard,
who supports my efforts
and encourages me to reach
for my dreams.

Foreword

Kohana was preparing for his first buffalo hunt. Evil dreams were destroying his self-confidence and making him afraid. Could he find anyone to help him before it was too late?

v

Contents

If you would like to have the authors of the Story Keeper Series visit your school free of charge, just call us at 1-800-321-5671 or 1-800-960-3876.

Dear Reader,

My name is Yuma. I am a Lakota Sioux. I am in third grade at Little Wound School in South Dakota. My school is on the Pine Ridge Reservation. My mother thinks that my skateboard will surely take root and grow to my feet. I think she exaggerates.

I study reading, science, and math, just like you. Spelling classes are different. I learn to spell *north* in English. I also learn the Lakota spelling: *wazi < yata*. Green is *zi to* and red is *'sa*. Will you come Friday and take my spelling test? I have Lakota culture classes, which is our religion.

Crazy Horse, a warrior, and Black Elk, a Holy Man, are two men of our tribe who are well known. Billy Mills is another famous Lakota. He won a gold medal in the 1964 Olympics. He was the first American to win the gold in the 10,000-meter race.

I hope you enjoy learning something about my people from this story. Our history is interesting and rich. The young Indian boy, Kohana, was my great-great-great-great-great-grandfather.

Yours truly,

Yuma

*   *   *   *   *   *   *   *   *   *

One

Dreams in the Night

I was falling! Down...down... down! There was nothing to grab! Down...down...down! Nothing but emptiness! Down...down...down!

"Wake up, Kohana." My big brother was shaking me. "Wake up."

Only a few coals from the fire pit dimly lit the tipi. I could see stars through the open smoke hole. Everyone was asleep except my brother, and now me.

"What happened?" I asked.

"You were dreaming," said my brother. "Are you all right?"

3

"Yes. Thank you," I answered. "Good night."

Dark surrounded me. But my memory pictured the arrow drawn on the outside of our tipi. It stood for my brave father's first buffalo hunt. A buffalo picture told of his victory. The tail from that buffalo hung inside the tipi. It was used to swat flies.

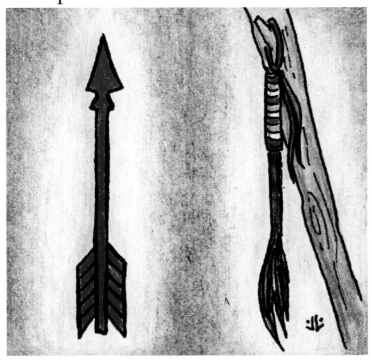

In three moons I would be old enough to go on my first hunt. My father had taught me how to make sharp flint arrowheads. We used a small hammer stone and a deer horn for chipping the arrowheads. They were fastened to long thin sticks.

"You make a fine arrowhead, my son," said my father. "Now let me show you how to make a spear. A buffalo is a big animal."

We made a spear much like the arrows, only bigger.

Already I had enough arrows and a fine bow for a hunt. I had a strong sharp spear. We were working on a knife. My father was looking forward to my first hunt.

How could I go on a hunt? It did not matter how many arrows and spears I had. I was not brave. A dream tossed my body like a feather. It caused me to kick out. It covered my body with sweat. Shame filled my heart.

When I was a baby, Mihigna ki, my grandmother, made a special amulet that she carefully hung from my cradleboard. The amulet had a lizard picture on it. The lizard was my guardian for a safe and long life. I wish I had it now.

Two

Cornbread from Chawee

Who would understand about my dreams? Who could help me? Father would be ashamed. Mama was too busy. Mihigna ki would scold, "You are too big and strong to be scared, Kohana." But I was scared. The dreams were bad.

My secret place was a curve in the creek. It was almost hidden from sight by a large rock and a clump of berry bushes.

I needed to think. I would hurry through my morning chores and slip away.

There I was. Lost in thought. All alone. What could I do? Softly a hand rested on my shoulder. I forgot that my sister Chawee and I share this quiet spot.

She was there. She sat down beside me. Without a word, she reached in the folds of her skirt. She handed me a piece of cornbread. It was still warm. How good it smelled. How good it felt to have Chawee beside me.

"I know," she said simply.

"Chawee, they are so bad!" I said. "There is evil in them."

"I know, my brother. And I know what we must do," she said. "I learned it from the Story Keeper at the Smudging Ceremony. She taught us about an old Lakota spiritual leader. He had a vision long ago when the world was young."

Chawee told the story. "Iktomi appeared to the leader in the form of a spider. He spoke about the cycles of life—how we begin as infants, then move on to childhood, then adulthood. Finally, we go to old age where we must be taken care of as infants, completing the cycle.

"As Iktomi spoke, he took the elder's willow hoop, which had beads, feathers, horsehairs, and offer-

ings on it. He began to spin a web.
He said that there are many forces in
each time of life. Some are good.
Some are bad.

"When Iktomi finished speaking and weaving, he gave the elder the web and said, 'The web is a perfect circle with a hole in the center. If you believe in the Great Spirit, the web will catch your good ideas. The bad ones will go through the hole.'

"Kohana, we will make a dream catcher to hang above your sleeping space," said Chawee. "The dream catcher will sift your dreams. The good will be captured to carry with you. The evil in your dreams will drop through the hole in the web and no longer be a part of your life."

"Did the Story Keeper tell you how to make a dream catcher, Chawee?" I asked.

"Yes," answered my sister. "Can you find a large circle? Maybe a large hollow bone or a gourd."

"I have a piece of backbone from a buffalo. I will smooth it down to a ring," I said. "What else?"

"I have the other things we need, except feathers," Chawee said.

"We can use my owl feathers. I have three," I offered.

Before it was time to sleep that night, a special dream catcher hung over my sleeping space. Somehow Chawee had added the perfect object. From a soft elk-skin strip hung the charm from my cradleboard with the lizard picture!

"Pilamaya ye, Chawee," I said. "Thank you."

Then, before I entered the tipi that night, I faced the west, north, east, and south, the zenith above, and the nadir below to show my respect and thanks for the dream catcher.

That night the bad dreams sifted through the circle. They never reached me.

Three

Ready for the Hunt

In three moons I was ready for my first hunt. The dream catcher my sister made for me had stopped the evil dreams. My father had taught me how to make the weapons I would need. He taught me how to use them.

"There is another lesson you must learn well, my son," said my father. "Our people travel to stay near the buffalo herds. You will need a pony that you can ride."

My father gave me a pony as swift as the wind.

19

My father said, "You will go on hunts in new places where you could lose your way. Here in the sea of grass there are few landmarks to mark your place. Remember always to look to the zenith above to guide you. The sun and the other stars will help you find your way."

My father taught me to use the stars not only to guide me, but also to time my hunting. Stars of great importance are the Morning Star (Venus), Ursa Major (the Big Dipper), and the Pleiades. Then he told me how the "Seven Little Girls" (the Pleiades) were placed in the sky. All the other stars whirled around the polestar. It kept its place in the sky.

"The buffalo, the provider for life's needs, is connected with the creation of life," my father said.

"Always give thanks and never kill more than your needs. Now, my son, you are ready for your first hunt. The buffalo is large, strong, and very fast. You must be brave and quick."

Chawee was waiting for me outside our tipi the day of the hunt. She was holding something in her hand.

"Bend down, my brave brother," she said. "I have something to keep you safe on this hunt."

When I knelt down in front of her, she placed the lizard charm around my neck. I felt safe. "I will bring you something special from my first hunt, Chawee," I said.

We were off! This was the day I had waited for all my life! I rode beside my father. How proud I felt to be a Lakota. We share the Earth as equal partners with our animal relatives, especially the buffalo.

When a herd was spotted, we did not go near at first. This was a large herd. My father said we would not surround the herd and kill them all. We would stampede the animals. Then each hunter was to separate the animal he wished to kill.

Buffalo do not hear well, but they smell very well. My father checked the direction of the wind. He signaled the others to follow him. The hunting party made a wide sweeping curve to the north side of the herd. Each pony and rider lined up side by side.

My heart was racing. My father raised his arm. All was quiet.

Down came my father's arm. Each horse sprang forward as we rushed headlong at the big herd of buffalo scattering at the charge.

There was shouting, yelling, and a loud thundering of hooves. Buffalo ran this way and that. When I spotted one near the edge of a crowd, I dashed my pony between it and the herd. The animal ran away from the others. I darted after it and shot arrow after arrow into its side.

The confusion and uproar did not last long. Then there he lay.

My father walked up by my side. We looked at my first buffalo. He put his arm on my shoulder. We gave thanks for the buffalo.

"Well done, my son," he said. "I believe your buffalo is bigger than mine!"

We waited for the women to arrive. They would skin and butcher the animals. My mother asked if there was any part of my first buffalo I wanted to keep.

"Yes, Mother," I said. "I want to keep the tongue to make Chawee a beautiful hairbrush from the rough side. I will make it the prettiest brush she has ever had!"

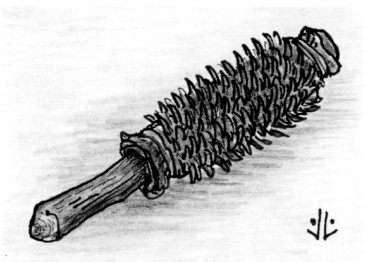

Chawee smiled. Holding my charm, I smiled back.

Four

Lakota Facts

Lakota Sioux
war shield

Lakota Sioux
tepee

Smallpox

Many buffalo

Peace with the Crows

Sitting Bull

Many buffalo

No food to eat

Symbol and sign:
to hear or listen

Symbol and sign:
to see or look

A hand painted on the face means he killed an enemy barehanded. A split feather means he was wounded many times. An eagle feather with four spots means he killed four of the enemy.

Spots are for coups against the enemy.

Four notches in feather: fourth
to wound an enemy

One notch with red mark: cut
the throat and scalped enemy

Face paint: vengeance and war

Sign language: horse

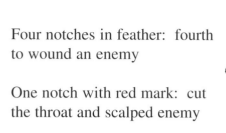

Buffalo

Horse

Horizontal eagle feather:
wearer counted second
coup.

Lightning stripes on face
indicate power.

Sign language: buffalo

Beyond "The End"

● Have you ever had a dream that scared you, like Kohana's? Write your dream in a few sentences, using a lot of descriptive adjectives.

● When you have finished writing about your dream, change the scary adjectives to pleasant adjectives. Does the dream sound as scary now? Adjectives are powerful words!

● Think of an adjective to make a perfect match with these nouns: dancer, cornbread, dreams, buffalo, warrior, and tipi.

CURRICULUM CONNECTIONS

● The Lakota used the stars to guide them in finding their way and to time their hunting, gathering, and ritual activities. Kohana learned to recognize the constellations and to use them as a map. Observe, record, and share your observations of the daytime sky. Do the same for the nighttime sky.

● Constellations, such as the Big Dipper, have many different myths from different cultures associated with them. Become acquainted with myths about the sun, the moon, and the stars.

● When ancient peoples observed the night skies, they saw what they called "wandering stars." What were the "wandering stars"?

● According to one Lakota legend, Fallen Star was the son of the North Star and a Lakota woman who lived in the Cloud World. Fallen Star and his mother fell to Earth from the clouds after his mother made a mistake. She tried to dig up a plant that was growing in the Cloud World—something she had been warned against. The North Star now broods all alone over the loss of his beloved Lakota wife and son.

● Write your own myth about why the North Star stands in the sky all alone.

THE ARTS

● Learn more about dream catchers and how to make your own at website: <www.teachersfirst.com/summer/dreamcatcher.htm>.

● Choose your favorite constellation. Cut out both ends of an empty frozen juice can. Place one end of the can on black construction paper. Trace a circle around the can, then cut out a circle about 1/2 inch larger than the circle you drew. Use a white colored pencil to make dots inside the circle, representing stars in your constellation. Using a small nail for large stars and a large pin for small stars, punch holes through the white dots. Glue or tape the black circle on one end of the juice can. Hold it up to a light to see your constellation!

GATHERING INFORMATION

● You can gather information by observation. Be a good observer. Notice things closely and carefully. These strategies will help:

1. Know why you are observing.
2. Use all your senses—look, listen, smell, touch, and taste.
3. Concentrate—block out other thoughts.
4. Think about what things mean.
5. Observe things from different places and angles.
6. Use your pencil to help you see—describe it (take notes) or sketch it.

THE BEST I CAN BE

● A Lakota prayer speaks of "beauty above me, beauty below me, beauty in me, and beauty all around me." Go outside. Look up—really look! Write about the beautiful things you see. Look down. Write about the beautiful things you see. Look inside you. Write about the things people who love you see as beautiful and the things you believe are beautiful, inside you. Look all around you. Write about the beautiful things.

● Learn to immerse yourself in nature. Its beauty can calm your anger, soothe hurt feelings, and erase worries. The more you look for and appreciate the beauty in nature, the more aware you will become of your responsibility to protect it.